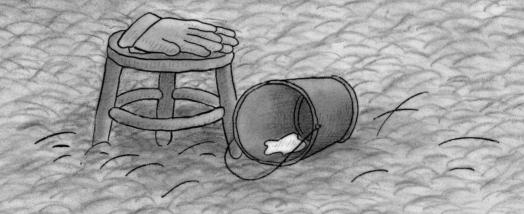

POST CARD

9:00 PM
1916

Library of Congress
Cataloging-in-Publication Data
Ernst, Lisa Campbell.
When Bluebell sang.
Summary: Bluebell the cow's talent
for singing brings her stardom but she
soon longs to be back at the farm—
if she can get away from her greedy manager.
[1. Cows—Fiction] I. Title. PZ7.E7323 Wh 1989
[E] 88-22262   ISBN 0-02-733561-5

Bradbury Press
An affiliate of Macmillan, Inc.
866 Third Avenue
New York, New York
10022

Collier Macmillan Canada, Inc.
Printed and bound in Japan
First American Edition
10 9 8 7 6 5 4 3 2 1

For Sharon

When
Bluebell
Sang

by Lisa Campbell Ernst

Bradbury Press   New York

On hot summer days, cows
often gather in the shade of large trees. Most people think
they are there to stay cool. The real story, though,
all begins with a cow named Bluebell.

Long ago when she was young, Bluebell seemed no different from any other cow.

She lived peacefully for years with a farmer named Swenson, his wife, Hazel, and the usual collection of farm animals.

One day, though, on his way to the barn, Swenson heard beautiful singing. "What's this?" he asked, opening the door. "Who's there?"

"It's me," Bluebell said, and then she began to sing again. Her voice was sweet and clear.

"Merciful heaven!" Swenson whispered. He ran to get his wife.

"Ya," Hazel said, hearing Bluebell. "It is the most beautiful singing I have ever heard."

Excited, Swenson loaded Bluebell onto the back of his wagon and headed for town. "Go ahead, Blue," he said proudly when they arrived.

Again, Bluebell sang.

With the very first note, an astonished crowd began to gather. "Wonderful!" they whispered. "Magnificent!" No one had ever heard such magical songs before. They gave everyone goose bumps.

At dusk, Swenson said he and Bluebell had to go home.

"Please, Mr. Swenson," the mayor urged, "will you bring your amazing cow to the music hall on Saturday? We must hear her again."

Swenson looked at Bluebell.

"My pleasure," she replied.

Swenson's cow, "Bluebell" to sing at Music Hall Saturday

News of Bluebell swept all through the town.

The mayor wrote his brother, a talent agent named Big Eddie, in Duluth. "Incredible," he said. "Come quick."

Big Eddie did just that.

On Saturday, watching as Bluebell dazzled her audience, Big Eddie couldn't believe his good fortune. Who would expect such a voice from a stupid cow, he thought.

As the curtain closed, Big Eddie rushed to meet Swenson and Bluebell. "Come with me," he said. "I'll make you rich! You'll see the world!"

Bluebell was speechless. First the concert, the applause, and now this, the chance of a lifetime. "It might be fun to travel," she finally whispered.

"We sure could use the extra money," Swenson added.

"We could be gone only a little while," they said together. "About a month."

"Sure," Big Eddie quickly agreed, "whatever you say."

NORTH CENTRAL LINE

Bags packed, the threesome left for Chicago the next day.

Big Eddie took charge immediately. "We have to do something about the way you look," he said to Bluebell. "No highbrow theater is going to welcome a fat country cow."

In Chicago he took her to a dressmaker. Bluebell had never worn a dress before. Or a hat. Or shoes.

"These shoes feel a little tight," Bluebell said, wincing. "Maybe my hooves could just be shined?"

"Look, *cow*." Big Eddie sneered. "We do things my way." Then he smiled and said, "I'm going to make you a star."

Bluebell and Swenson felt very faraway from home.

Everything happened just the way Big Eddie said it would.

Bluebell sang in concert halls, theaters, and auditoriums, at parties, street fairs, and department stores. She sang anywhere Big Eddie could get people to pay money to hear her sing. Weeks passed.

Wherever they went, crowds gathered. Reporters followed them endlessly.

There was no doubt Bluebell was a star.

From Chicago they traveled to Philadelphia, and then to New York. As their journey away from the farm grew to months, Bluebell and Swenson became homesick.

Now, napping, Bluebell dreamed about the farm fields, fresh and sunny. She sleepily switched her tail to brush away the lazy flies.

Swenson, too, was weary. He missed Hazel, and taking care of the animals. He found himself looking for farming articles in the local newspapers.

One night Bluebell and Swenson went to see Big Eddie. "We've traveled much longer than a month," Swenson said. "We must go home now."

Big Eddie's face turned red. "After all I've done for you," he shouted, "you can't quit now—I have plans, big plans!"

Bluebell and Swenson didn't know what to do. They had never seen Big Eddie so angry.

"Okay," Bluebell said at last, "one more month. Then we have to go home."

Big Eddie laughed. "Sure," he said, "whatever you say."

Dear Hazel,
Big Eddie has asked us to stay one more month. We miss you very much. Today

From New York they traveled to Boston, with stops all along the way.

So many concerts made Bluebell even more famous, and even more tired. Now each dress she wore started new fashion trends, every song she sang became a hit.

And the more money Big Eddie made, the greedier he became.

"Don't worry, Blue," Swenson would say each night, "we'll be home soon. Big Eddie promised."

At the end of the month, Swenson and Bluebell went to remind Big Eddie that it was time to go home.

From outside his door, they heard him speaking loudly on the phone. "Don't worry," he was saying. "The cow and her stupid friend won't be a problem. They'll keep touring as long as I say so. I'll never let them go." Big Eddie's laugh was mean and nasty.

Bluebell and Swenson tiptoed back to their room.

"We're going to have to sneak out and buy our tickets for home," Bluebell said at last, "before Big Eddie can stop us."

Swenson turned white. "But, Blue," he said, "we don't have nearly enough money. Big Eddie hasn't paid us a cent."

Bluebell sat down to think.

The following morning Bluebell met Big Eddie for breakfast.

"I've been thinking, Ed," Bluebell said. "This concert life is great. I don't ever want to quit!"

Big Eddie had never looked happier. "At last you see things my way," he replied.

Bluebell smiled sweetly. "I have a great plan," she said, "that should make us both a lot of money."

Big Eddie leaned forward to listen.

"The first thing we do is go back to Swenson's farm," Bluebell whispered.

The next day, Bluebell's upcoming visit to her home was big news.

Big Eddie was quoted for the details: After allowing reporters to tour the farm, Miss Bluebell would reveal a long list of concerts planned for the West Coast.

"What a terrific idea she had," Big Eddie muttered. "With all this publicity, the West Coast tickets will be sold out! I'll be even richer!"

When Swenson, Bluebell, and Big Eddie finally arrived at the farm, reporters were waiting. Big Eddie excitedly rushed to meet them.

In the hubbub, Bluebell silently slipped away.

As Big Eddie tried to organize the crowd, people called out, "We want to talk to Bluebell! Where is she?"

Big Eddie looked around. Then he saw Swenson pointing to the barn. "What is she doing in there?" he asked angrily. "She's supposed to be here, ready for pictures."

Big Eddie marched over and opened the barn doors.

"Bluebell!" he shouted. "Bluebell!" Big Eddie walked inside.

A sea of black and white cows stared back at him.

"She's not here!" Big Eddie called out. But then he saw something on the ground.

It was a dress, with a hat and shoes.

Big Eddie looked again at the crowd of cows. He tried to laugh. "Stop fooling around, Blue," he said. "Come on out."

There was no answer.

By this time, Swenson, Hazel, and a group of
reporters were at the door.

"These cows all look the same to me!" Big Eddie
yelled. "Which one is she?"

Swenson said he didn't know.

Now Big Eddie was desperate. "Okay!" he shouted.
"All you cows line up." The cows did as they were told.

Big Eddie marched by them, one by one.

"Sing!" he commanded.

"Moooooo," each cow sang.

When Bluebell's turn came, Swenson held his breath.
Bluebell paused and opened her mouth.

Out came a gloriously ear-splitting
"MOOOOOOOOOOOO."

Big Eddie didn't give her a second glance.

After a few days, Big Eddie gave up and went back to Duluth.

Bluebell, of course, continued her singing. She performed for her friends on the farm and taught the other cows how to sing as well.

Those cows taught their children and their grandchildren. But first they would tell the story of Bluebell, Swenson, and Big Eddie. Then they would give this advice: "When you sing, go out in the field, in the shade of a large tree. No one will suspect a thing."

On quiet summer days when the breeze carries sound, you might hear them still.

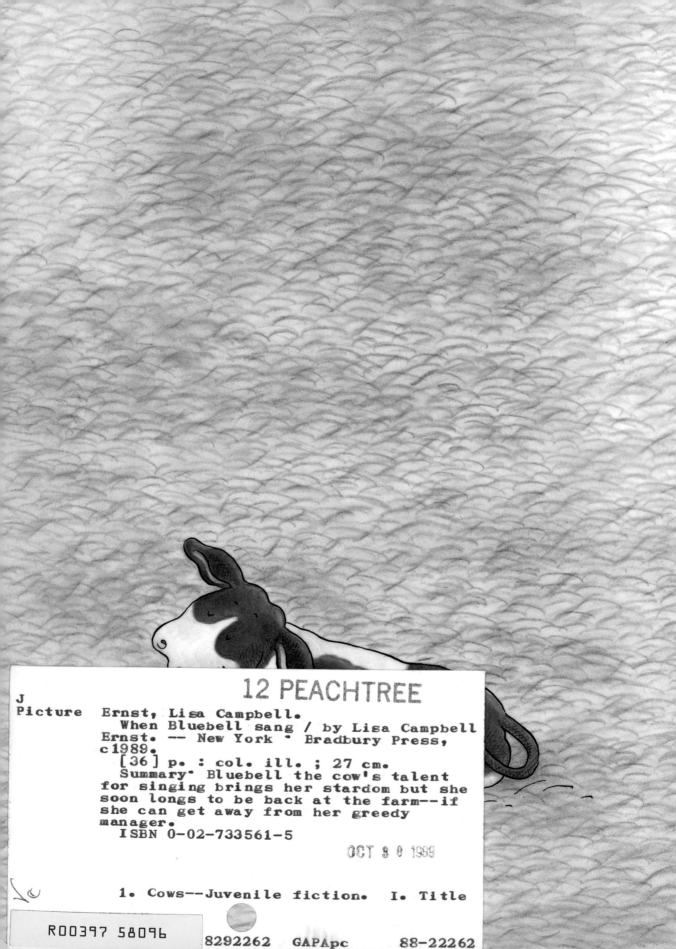